FOR MY GRANDCHILDREN, CAROLYN ROSE,
JACOB BOWMAN, AND AVA RAE- AND ALL OF THOSE
IN THE COMING GENERATIONS OF STORYTELLERS
-JB

FOR MY LOVES AT HOME.
NOTHING ELSE MATTERS
-DD

Reycraft Books
55 Fifth Avenue
New York, NY 10003
Reycraftbooks.com

Reycraft Books is a trade imprint and trademark of Newmark Learning, LLC.

Text copyright © 2020 by Joseph Bruchac
Illustration copyright © 2020 by Reycraft Books

Educators and Librarians: Our books may be purchased in bulk for promotional,
educational, or business use. Please contact sales@reycraftbooks.com.

This is a work of fiction. Names, characters, places, dialogue, and
incidents described either are the product of the author's imagination or are used
fictitiously. Any resemblance to actual persons, living or dead, is entirely coincidental.

Sale of this book without a front cover or jacket may be unauthorized. If this book is
coverless, it may have been reported to the publisher as "unsold or destroyed" and
may have deprived the author and publisher of payment.

Library of Congress Cataloging-in-Publication Data is available.

ISBN: 978-1-4788-6870-5

Printed in Guangzhou, China. 4401/0520/CA22000799
10 9 8 7 6 5 4 3 2 1

First Edition Hardcover published by Reycraft Books

Reycraft Books and Newmark Learning, LLC, support diversity and the First
Amendment, and celebrate the right to read.

THE POWWOW TREASURE

BY **JOSEPH BRUCHAC**

ILLUSTRATED BY **DALE DEFOREST**

JUST IN TIME

Drops of rain hit Jamie's face. *Why did I go out in the rain without an umbrella?* he thought. Then he felt the pillow under his head.

Wait a minute! I'm in bed.

He opened his eyes in time to see the next drop of water falling from the glass held over his head.

His twin sister smiled.

STOP IT!

COME ON, LITTLE BROTHER. GET UP. MAYBE WE SHOULD CHANGE YOUR NAME TO RIP VAN WINKLE.

Jamie Longbow looked at the clock on the trailer wall.

I'VE READ THAT STORY. RIP VAN WINKLE SLEPT FOR YEARS. I'VE ONLY BEEN SLEEPING FOR EIGHT HOURS.

OVERSLEEPING. GRAMA AND GRAMPA NEED YOUR HELP SETTING UP. THE POWWOW IS GOING TO START SOON. LISTEN!

Jamie could feel the beat of the drums and hear singing in the distance. The two drum groups were warming up. He was late. It would be time for Grand Entry soon.

He threw off the covers, jumped up, and landed with both feet inside his sneakers.

HUNH? I DON'T NEED TO. I GOT UP EARLY. EARLY ENOUGH TO SWITCH YOUR SNEAKERS AROUND.

TA-DA! I BET YOU CAN'T DO THAT, BIG SISTER.

Jamie looked down. His right sneaker was on his left foot. His left sneaker was on his right foot. "I look like a bear," he laughed.

Marie laughed with him. They had learned animal tracking from their father. They knew bears have their big toes on the outside of their feet.

Jamie switched his sneakers, and they both raced to the booth. Grampa Longbow stood on a small ladder. He stretched the canvas roof into place.

"Just in time, Grandson," he said. "Hand me those tie-downs one by one."

"You see," Jamie whispered to Marie. "I'm not late. I'm just in time."

Marie waved him away. Then she helped Grama
arrange her beading things. Today she would sit next to
Grama. Both of them would be making beaded bracelets.
*Will there be another mystery to solve at this
powwow?* she wondered.

2
LESTER LAUGHING

A tall man wearing full regalia approached the booth. His regalia was the old kind. Not fancy dance regalia with many colors—no bright tones like fire red and forest green and golden yellow. It was the men's traditional style with buckskin. He carried a big eagle feather fan. He had a large scar next to his nose. But his face was friendly.

He looked at them with a wide grin.

Jamie and Marie had never seen him before, but they smiled back.

"You must be the twins," he said. "You two running this booth now?"

"Our grandparents had to get some things from our trailer," Jamie said. "We're just holding the fort."

The man chuckled. It was a deep chuckle from way down in his big belly. "Holding the fort?" he asked. "Are you worried about an Indian attack?"

Jamie felt silly. Then he laughed, too. So did Marie. The tall man was just teasing the way Grampa Longbow did.

Marie looked down politely as she answered. It was good manners to look down when you were being complimented.

A NEW MYSTERY

Marie was so excited she could hardly talk. A new mystery? Was it about something stolen—like the bracelet the raven took?

Jamie was excited, too. Maybe this time he could solve the mystery before his sister. He also wondered how Mr. Laughing heard about them. The stolen bracelet had happened in Massachusetts. Now they were in Connecticut.

Lester Laughing leaned close. "One thing, though," he whispered. "Don't tell your grampa and grama till you solve the mystery."

"Why?" Marie asked.

"So it will be a surprise."

Lester Laughing pulled a brown envelope from the deerskin pouch at his waist. He leaned over and put it on the table.

The man laughed a deep laugh, both hands on his big stomach.

"Because I chose you," he said. He lifted his eagle feather fan and touched it to each of their foreheads. "You will do good," he said.

Then he turned and vanished into the crowd.

Jamie opened the flap of the envelope.

Marie reached inside. She pulled out a folded piece of deerskin and put it onto the table.

Jamie unfolded it.

"Wow!" he said. The deerskin looked very old. It had words written on it in dark ink.

T FIND TREZUR.
START AT BIG WITE RCK.
LOOK T WINTR
FROM ITS TOP.

There were more words, but . . . .

Jamie shoved the deerskin map back into the envelope. Then he stuck the envelope under the cushion of the folding chair he'd been sitting on.

Grampa sat on the chair where the map was hidden.

Grampa got up from the chair. "Boy," he said, "this chair feels sort of stiff."

Marie pulled up another chair. "Here, Grampa. This one is better."

While Grampa was sitting, Jamie picked up the pillow and the envelope with the map.

"I'll get another pillow," he said. He took the pillow and envelope behind the wall of the booth. He pulled out the map and put it into his shirt.

THE BIG WHITE ROCK

At first, the words on the map were hard to understand.

"What is a 'wite rck'?"

"I know," Marie said. "Look over there."

At the edge of the powwow grounds sat a huge white stone.

"Whoever wrote this can't spell," Jamie said.

The twins climbed on top of the big white rock.

"What now?" Jamie asked.

Marie read more of the instructions.

LOOK T WINTR
GO T CRSS

"Winter," Jamie said. "We have to look north."

They both turned to the north. A hundred yards away they could see an old tree. Its top was broken off and it had only two limbs sticking out.

"CRSS must mean cross. That's it," Jamie said. "That's the cross."

They hopped off the rock and ran to the tree.

"Now what?" Jamie asked.

The two of them looked at the map.

TRN T SMMR
GO T TREE
DIG AT ONE
T TREZUR SEE

"That must be summer. South. Whoever wrote this sure doesn't like vowels," Jamie said. They both looked south. Then they looked at each other. There were no trees, just a wide field with a stone wall around it.

ONE, TWO, THREE

"Did someone cut down all the trees?" Jamie asked. He walked over to the stone wall. He ran his hands over the stones. Was there something in the rocks? Writing, maybe? Or the shape of a tree? He couldn't see anything unusual.

Marie studied the rocks in the wall, too. Then she turned around in a circle, seeking some sort of clue. But there seemed to be nothing around to help them.

They sat and looked at the map again.

LET'S THINK ABOUT THIS.

Marie looked where Jamie pointed.
There were three places on the wall
where stones had been piled up to
make towers.

They ran to the wall and dug at the base
of the first stone tower. There they found
an old metal box twice as big as a shoebox.

Both Grama and Grampa were at the booth when the twins returned.

Marie held out the box.

WE FOUND A BURIED TREASURE. HERE.

WHERE HAVE YOU BEEN? YOU'RE BOTH COVERED IN DIRT.

Grampa and Grama took the box. The cover was rusted shut. Grampa grabbed his tools and pried it open with a big screwdriver.

OH. MY.

THAT'S A TREASURE FOR SURE. LOOK, GRANDCHILDREN.

Jamie and Marie looked into the box. It was not full of gold and silver coins like a pirate's treasure. It was full of something better. It held hundreds of old purple and white wampum beads. They could be used to make so many beautiful things.

"Where'd you find this?" Grampa asked.

Jamie handed him the map. "Mr. Laughing gave this to us."

"Lester Laughing?" Grama asked. A funny look swept over her face.

UNHN-HUNH. HE SAID HE CHOSE US TO FIND THE TREASURE.

BIG MAN WITH A SCAR ALONG THE SIDE OF HIS NOSE?

YES.

HE SAID HE WAS AN OLD FRIEND OF OUR FAMILY.

HE SURE WAS. AND HE LIVED AROUND HERE.

HE MADE THE BEST THINGS FROM WAMPUM. MADE EVERY BEAD BY HAND.

Meet
JOSEPH BRUCHAC

I'm a writer and traditional storyteller. An enrolled member of the Nulhegan Band of the Abenaki Nation, I've performed as a storyteller and sold books and my own crafts at northeastern powwows since the early 1980s. My family and I run the annual Saratoga Native American Festival in Saratoga Springs, New York. One of my favorite powwow memories is when I was honored with a blanket at the Shelburne Museum powwow in Vermont twenty years ago.

Meet
DALE DEFOREST

I was born in Tuba City, Arizona, but raised on the Navajo Reservation in northwestern New Mexico. My mother says I've been an illustrator since I was able to hold a crayon. I used to lie on my back and draw pictures under the coffee table in my parents' living room. Apart from being an illustrator, I'm a storyteller, graphic designer, and musician. I reside in Albuquerque, New Mexico, and am a happily married father of two. Anything and everything I do, I do for my loved ones. The ultimate goal of my career is to do what I do, from the comfort of my home. Several of the characters depicted in this adorable story were inspired by loved ones in my own life, namely my mother, sister, and brother.